I0830731

Little Mirror

By Josephine J. Bridgers

Little Mirror

by Josephine Jenkins

copyright 2011

Revised 2019

Josephine Jenkins Bridgers

Front book covering artwork and design by Jamil Burton and Denise Sharpe

I would like to thank Lonnie Parker and David Jones for proofing Little Mirror.

I thank God for his mercy and glory! Included on my journey is my family: Calvin Bridgers, Larry Hill, Michael Hill, Kimberly Hill, Lillian Jenkins, Earnest Jenkins, Carylon Fields and Bettie Harrison, these are the people that stood behind me

Little Mirror by Josephine J. Bridgers

Table of Content

WHEN THERE IS LIFE, THERE IS HOPE

Prologue

Oh, the rain was pouring down and lightning was shooting by during the fight to become the next mirror. This time, the mirror returned and landed on the shadow of the little runt. The bid for Little Mirror had already been selected. But who, and where? Only the signs in heavens had the clue.

As the rain danced in place, the skies opened up and rainbows of all colors shot passed everyone in the Land of Dreams and landed near the little runt.

The earth was in trouble, evilness had become an epidemic. To rid the earth of evil, this battle would entail a brave being filled with the diversities of a warrior and the soul of a hero. Could this fight be won? It depended on this runt. Nevertheless, the little runt was willing to take on this battle, because the Earth's survival rested on his shoulders. Boy, he was ready to prove to all the bullies that he was worthy of this honor.

"I will take on the battle," the brave little runt said, "I will become Little Mirror!"

His father looked cautious, while his mother smiled. "Yes, my baby is the one, the smallest and the humblest being of all. He will become Little Mirror! Normally, it would've been the woman in the Land of Dreams to choose the next Little Mirror, but due to the significance of the task, a higher power had selected the next Little Mirror. But the little runt had to prove he was worthy by completing the final test. He had to outrun several contenders and break through the walls of several mirrors and reclaim the seal. Next, he had to place the seal on his forehead where the word "Burden" was forming.

The beings from the Land of Dreams secretly thought, the little runt would fail because every race the little runt ran in, he had fell behind and was the last one.

His mother smiled. "You can do it my son! 'now go!"

The little runt ran forward, now he would prove to all the bullies who picked on him that this honor was his. Because of his size, he was shunned by all the larger contenders.

The little runt ran and ran.

He caught up with the biggest contender, Mojo. Mojo looked confused, did this little runt just pass me? He thought. The little runt continued outrunning all his contenders; he knew he needed to retrieve the seven mirrors and fast before the rainbows settled back in the sky. He jumped high in the sky catching all seven mirrors with his toes. Then, he whirled them around and around until the colors of the rainbow opened the protected covering. This allowed him to dive into each mirror, one by one and retrieve the hidden seal located in the inner crack of the last mirror. He had to do it without breaking any of the mirrors. When the little runt emerged, he had the seal, but he had to run through some bad dreams and lift their burdens before he would be accepted as the next Mirror. He stumped his feet, and a river was formed; he blew his breathe, and there was a massive windstorm.

He battled the creepiest dream and dissembled it, then he scooped up all its elements and formed a tunnel sealing it in a capsule surrounded by one bad no-nonsense rainbow. The other contenders gave off a sigh because they were sure the runt would fail, and they would become the next mirror.

Then the little runt's father stepped forward.

His father spoke softly, scrutinizing the little runt up and down. Then, he said, "little one, you know if you don't win this battle, dreams will be destroyed forever." "Yes, my father," the runt replied.

His father camouflaged the frame of the mirror with webs making it look old and dingy. The webs would trap the burden and bind it. The dinginess would blind the enemies and keep them from getting close to the mirror. Then, the little runt's father mixed a mixture of hazelnuts and berries. This was a very nauseating odor. It was so strong it would overwhelm the little runt's enemies preventing them from attacking him.

"Go, my son," Little Mirror's father said, "fight and be victorious!" Little Mirror gave his father a Power Hug. This was a symbol of respect in the Land of Dreams. A Power Hug was when a mirror materialized.

Now, Little Mirror was on his way to the earth, on his wings made from dreams.

The Early Stages of Little Mirror

Flames of fury, balls of fire, hail and lightning appeared as the heavens opened, dividing the seasons; spring, winter, summer and fall. The great Earth would never forget this day.

It was a day when darkness and light seemed to collide in the sky; a day when every being was gazing upward, afraid to challenge the sights before their eyes.

Look! The stars were dancing clockwise in the sky. Then, all the clouds came together and sealed off the lights from all eyes. There was only blackness. Darkness covered the sky for miles and miles. Creatures far and wide gathered their mates while they lifted their eyes to this unbelievable sight. They were terrified. They had never seen anything like this before.

Suddenly, there was an explosion. It was a force greater than deer rattling their horns. Boom! Boom! The sounds were heard far and wide. It was worse than the most frightening thunderstorm with all the giant-sized hail that rained down on the unsuspecting animals.

Then, finally, emerging from the light, a figure pierced the darkness as he divided the clouds. It was an indistinct creature. No one could tell what it was. It landed, burning in flames, enclosed in a mucous wrapped vest. The figure was woven in a spider web. The image was blurry with no distinct features and it was attached to the frame of a mirror.

The being seemed to have a shadow within its frame. When the being fell, it landed on the highest mountain. But, strangely, it started to roll backwards. It continued to move downward for hours. When the being finally came to rest, it was in a garden where Momma and Papa Rays resided. It was at that moment Little

Mirror, the strange looking being, was adopted by Momma and Papa Rays. They nurtured and sheltered him through the early stages of his life and gave him the glow of light that reflected through his frame.

His new parents were rays of light that beamed down from heaven. They shined their light rays over all the greeneries in the rainforest, and in each beam were the colors of the rainbow: red, orange, yellow, green, blue and purple.

But the older Little Mirror got, he questioned why he looked so different from Momma and Papa Ray. Momma Ray took a long contemplative pause, and finally concluded it was time to tell him the truth. "It began," she started, "with a strange sound heard across the universe. Wham! Boom! Boom! Thunderous sounds, as flakes of clouds encircled the sky. Then down you fell, landing in our garden." "But where did I come from?" Little Mirror asked excitedly. His surrogate mother replied, "I don't know the answer to all the questions, but you came from a distant place where beings of this world have never ventured. There was lightning, thunder, and rain flowing like feathers in the sky," she continued much to the delight of Little Mirror. "First, you were swept on the surface of the mountain top surrounded by lava dripping from your frame. That lava was so hot it burned miles and miles of trees, but on you it didn't even cause a sweat. On your back is engraved the word Burden, but I do not know what it means." Little Mirror sat back in awe to take it all in.

As the years passed, Little Mirror grew with lightning speed. His appearance had changed, and his hormones seemed to be running wild. Bright colors seemed to follow him everywhere he went. The rainbow that Momma and Papa Rays had told him about that was on his back began to throb over the inscription Burden, and neither Momma nor Papa Ray could explain why.

Little Mirror now felt it was time for him to venture out on his own. One day, Little Mirror came upon a sly fox. He had heard stories about how cunning the fox was from the other animals. Edging closer, he sat and listened because this animal amazed him.

Little Mirror also remembered when he was just a babe that this same fox had tried to get him to come closer so that he could snatch him. Momma Ray rescued him from this hideous plight. Momma Ray sent a ray of fire to the fox's behind.

When Little Mirror got older, he had another bad experience with the fox. Because this creature thought he could outsmart everyone in the forest, the fox told Little Mirror that he was looking after the little rabbits. Instead, the fox was trying to get the little rabbits to come out of their hiding place so he could feast on them. Even though Little Mirror was small, he asked the sly fox, "Do you think I'm a fool?" Little Mirror had to teach this cunning fox a lesson about humility, because at the time the fox would tell a lie while professing it was the truth. To make matters worse, this animal sounded so believable. When someone chased after the fox, this creature outran them every time.

In the fox's cave, there were stacks of food. He was prepared for everything. He was prepared for snowstorms, for the summer heat, and other disasters waiting to happen. He hoarded food. The farmer and his family were struggling to survive, but the fox didn't care. Self-preservation was all that mattered to him. It was all about him and his family.

Little Mirror asked the fox one day, "Why fox, are you hoarding so much food?" The sly fox replied, "Because I can! I need to get it while I can! Besides, no one can catch me, because boy I can fly!" Little Mirror tried reasoning with the fox, but the fox wouldn't listen. The fox became haughty, because after all, he knew the farmer couldn't outrun him.

Little Mirror got out his lasso made from rainbows, and he lassoed until all the rainbows returned to his holster, one by one. The rainbows flew fast towards the fox. The fox tried to run, but the rainbows caught up with him. One of the rainbows hit the fox right on top of his feet. "Ouch!" yelled the fox, "What was that?" The other rainbow slowed the fox down by putting trees in the fox's path. And before all the other animals' eyes, a transformation had started to occur. Colors were circling around the fox. Oh, what a magical sight! Then something started to change inside the fox, and he smiled. The fox now felt remorse for what he had put the other animals through, and he became very humble.

Years had passed and the fox had now gotten old. He couldn't run fast. Everyday pastimes such as stealing chicken became too much for him with his slow feet. The fox could barely walk.

Then one day, the fox was sitting down by the river weeping uncontrollably, because his feet were no longer fast enough to escape the farmer's wrath after catching his prey. Every time the fox tried to get food, he dropped whatever chicken he was carrying. The last time the fox tried to get chickens from the farmer's barn, the farmer caught up with him and almost broke his legs. Oh my, it was still hurting from when the farmer was swinging him around and around. Little Mirror, who was watching from nearby, felt sorry for the fox.

Little Mirror gathered all his rainbows together. He took out his favorite two and shot his bows right near the fox's feet. The bows of rainbows made swishing sounds. The fox's feet began to change into gigantic wings. Now, the fox had feet made of wings. The elated fox ran fast on his way to the farmer's barn.

The very next day, the fox went to get a feast from the farmer's chickens. After selecting two healthy looking birds, the fox's little feet flew away from the fury of the farmer's anger. The fox escaped to the safety of the forest. What a happy fox! Hooray!

Hooray! He was now able to supply his family with food, and his little ones flourished.

Little Mirror had rushed home to tell Momma and Papa Rays, but his story seemed so eccentric. It was hard for even them to believe. Little Mirror felt his back, unsure if what he remembered really happened, and for some reason his back felt a little different.

Weeks passed without an incident, so Little Mirror gave up trying to make a miracle happen. He wasn't in trouble and all the miraculous things that had occurred usually happened when someone was in trouble.

One day, a farmer was frantic because he had been hunting all day and he had not slayed anything. Little Mirror, standing right beside the farmer, saw his frustration. He knew the man had a big family to feed. Little Mirror stepped forward, whispering. His rainbows danced in place while he selected two that had lightning speed. Boom! Boom! Two rainbows flew past Little Mirror hitting a 150-pound deer. The deer was brownish with a fluffy white abdomen. The deer burst into the clearing. "Oh my," the hunter yelled out. Quickly, the farmer shot the deer. This deer provided enough to feed the farmer's household for days. His wife even made a stew from the lean portions.

Little Mirror rushed home again to tell Momma and Papa, but when he got there he decided to keep it to himself because he doubted they would believe him. Still he noticed his back felt a little bit heavier.

The child was lost in the forest

.

Then, one day, a child wandered into the woods crying his little heart out. "Where are my parents? Please help me. I'm lost and scared." The child bowed down on his knees and started sobbing again. Even though, Little Mirror was only a little babe himself, he felt sorry for the child.

"Stop! Stop!" Little Mirror said. It seemed like an eternity to the child, but to Little Mirror it was only a second. Boom! Boom! A narrow path formed through the woods with a big hand made from all the colors of the rainbow pointing the child in the direction that led him home to his fluffy pillow and a warm fireplace.

As time passed, word spread quickly of the miracles Little Mirror performed, and everyone began to seek him out to solve their problems. Momma and Papa had heard about it and called for Little Mirror. Upon seeing him, Momma Ray instantly noticed the difference on his back. The blurry image in the mirror had begun to have a little shape to it, but it was still indistinct. The most amazing thing though was Little Mirror's back, where the letters engraved ''Burden'' had a little bulge to it now. They asked Little Mirror to perform one of the miracles they had heard about, but no matter how hard Little Mirror tried he couldn't, because Mama and Papa Rays did not have any problems.

How the Lion became the King of the Jungle

Have you ever speculated how the lion became King of the Jungle? Well here is the story.

In a time when the lion soared about ten feet in height and weighed over 3000 pounds, this ferocious creature was a coward. Most of the animals in the forest were certainly much smaller than the lion, but they weren't afraid of this big scary cat. The smallest animals even picked at this oversized creature. His supremacy to rule the jungle was in question. How can you follow a coward? The lion couldn't even fend for himself or care for his little ones, because he lacked the most important quality of all. He lacked courage. At that time, it wasn't clear who ruled the forest. In fact, the lion was considered a vulture, because he only fed on the remains of carcasses that were left by the other animals. A notorious scavenger was what the lion was known as.

The lion dreamed of a day when he would be able to overpower the hippo. This dream evaporated into smoke because of the empty noise coming from his stomach. You see, the hippo was no easy target. It outweighed the lion weighing in at 7,000 pounds or more, and the hippo's skin was so thick that it made it impossible for any animal to tackle this piece of meat, let alone try to slaughter it. Another stumbling block was that the hippo was never alone. It usually traveled with a group. All the other animals were afraid, especially when the hippo yawned. The other animals, especially the lion, knew it was time to get out of the hippo's way. The hippo was bad. The hippo would pick up the other animals and throw them back and forth in the air. If the animals fell, oh well. Some of the animals got seriously hurt but this creature could care less. A little fun sometimes hurts.

Now, let's find out why the lion pitied himself. Here is his story, and how he became the King of the Jungle.

One day, the lion was thinking of how he could overpower the hippo. The lion was very apprehensive, and he lacked confidence. Little Mirror was standing next to the lion. He was identical to the big cat but with a glow that reflected like a mirror on his forehead.

Little Mirror "RRRRRRRRRRRRRRR... why, my big cat, don't you have any get up and go?" "I'm a loser," said the lion. "The hippo would be a sure meal, but I can't win that fight. It is sooooooo big. I'm afraid, but if I don't find food soon, I will perish. If I chase the hippo, he will certainly overpower me. I can outrun him, but he has the strength." With every hour passing, the lion was getting more famished. He paced, he trotted, he paced, and he trotted. "If I catch up with the hippo, it would take my teeth forever to dig into the hippo's skin. If only I could conquer my fear and stand firm and fight, I would gain the respect of the animals in the jungle. What's a creature like me to do?" "Stop!" Little Mirror said. "Stop! Be what you need to be," he said while he gracefully ran forward, unleashing the rainbow bolts, and shooting the bolts straight towards the lion. Zzzzzzzzzzzzzzzzzzzzzzzzzz bright colors, loud colors and mild colors, they all encircled the lion. Moving swiftly, before the lion could bat an eye, the rainbow engulfed every inch of the feline creature. The smoke caused the other animals to flee behind the trees. There were blue, yellow, gold, pink, orange rainbows, and the rainbows were ready to fight. After the smoke disappeared, walking through all the colors was the lion. He was transformed into one of the mighty creatures that ever graced the forest. The lion opened his mouth. Where there were small teeth, now there were fangs. They were razor sharp that could bite through the toughest skin. Even his coat had a majestic look, fitting for royalty. And when the lion roared, his voice shocked him. "Roarrrrrrrrrrrrrrrrrrrrrrrrrng ARrrrrrrrrrrrrrrrrrrrrrrrr!" Now with this voice, all the hippos would fear him. The lion's roar broke the threshold of time. It woke the bears that were hibernating, and all the birds fell from the sky. For that moment time stood still. Little Mirror got one of his favorite rainbows and shot it right at Father Time. "Go back" said Little Mirror, "it's not your time. The lion needs to complete his transformation before you make your entrance." The lion roaring said, "Is it really me, I'm beautiful." He looked down at his coat that once looked messy, now was lustrous, brownish and was shining like a newborn. The lion's feet were covered with claws that could rip the toughest skin to shreds. All the other animals stood in an awe state. The lion charged at the big hippo with full force. The hippo stopped laughing almost choking on his teeth that had fell out after he bumped into a tree. The hippo started to run. "HA, HA, YOU'RE NOT LAUGHING NOW!" yelled the Lion.

The lion stood on his back legs beating his chest. The smaller animals started to come closer but slower. Little Mirror, identical to the cat, was standing on the opposite side. Now, Little Mirror said, "It's time for you to fight for honor and power. 'Goooooooooo now! Show you're the rightful king of the Jungle!"

After chasing the hippo for a while, the lion caught up with the hippo and planted his fangs that were protruding from his mouth into the hippo's neck.

This battle created rivers and cleared green lands where trees were plentiful. Now there was an empty space. There had never been a battle like this before. This was a battle for strength, power, and the right to rule the jungle.

But this day, the lion was victorious. The hippo and his group fled howling like wolves bumping into each other. The other animals were happy because they didn't like the big ole hippo anyway.

Now was the time to show his authority. The lion challenged all.

"Ha, ha, I am what was needed to be the rightful King of the Jungle. The one that was, the one now to be, the rightful heir!

Gruuuuuuuuuuuuuuuuuuuuuuuuuuuuuuu!

Little Alligator

Little Mirror was still struggling through his adolescent stage; he had bumps everywhere. Papa Ray had to have a little talk with him about the changes he was experiencing. But enough of that, Little Mirror had a bigger problem; he had to do something about the prickly alligator.

Would you believe there was one creature who Little Mirror despised? Yes, it was the prickly and mischievous alligator. Little Mirror could deal with all the other creatures, but not this creature. The alligator was so self-indulged he lacked empathy. He boasted about his conquests saying, "There are no other creatures as crafty as me." Roaming the land, he was a pest to all the other animals. Most of the animals secretly wanted this troublemaker gone. Not knowing this, the alligator thought that all the other animals loved him. Sure, he tore up their homes, but to him it was all in fun. So what he planted his big body on top of the smaller animals until they passed out, it was all play time for him. Everyday this creature would sneak up on the little rabbits and little birds while they were relaxing under the trees from the summer heat. Panic stricken, the animals almost passed out, because they were truly afraid. They didn't like the prickly alligator playing tricks on them. "Ha, ha," he laughed. "It's just me," the alligator said. Nevertheless, the animals remained hidden. Secretly, all the other animals loathed the alligator. At that time, the alligator could change his colors to blend in with all the greenery in the forest.

Finally, Little Mirror had enough. He heard the cries of all the animals and knew it was time to act. "Such nonsense will stop," Little Mirror said. Boom! Rainbows shot forth. They covered the entire land. The rainbows covered the prickly alligator's skin. His skin became scaly with his body stretching over ten feet. Even his demeanor changed, causing him to look creepy and unrecognizable. He became very hard on the eyes, and he rarely came on land. The animals were thrilled. The troublemaker no longer caused them much grief. The other animals cheered!

Poor alligator, he has only himself to blame for his appearance

One reason why the Bears hibernate in the winter

Little Mirror was growing up fast; his hormones were causing him to sweat all over his mirror. Caught up in his on growing pain, he forgot to check on the bears and this caused a devastation that he was not prepared for.

In winter, a significant part of the bear population had died. At one point in time, the bear was the most feared animal. It dominated the land. But the winter months were causing hardships for the bears, and they were becoming an endangered species. This winter was the worst. It was one of the coldest winters ever. The bears were struggling to survive. This winter the snow had piled up almost ten feet with massive flakes covering the earth for miles and miles. Every crack and every corner were covered in flakes. Food was nowhere to be found. There were thousands of bears probing to find a warm spot, but all the places they came upon were inhabited by other animals. Bears young and old were dying like flies. The pack had a handful left before one mother cried out in pain, "Please, please help us, my cubs are dying, my mate is gone." Little Mirror came closer to see the devastation. He smelled the aroma of blood. It had a foul odor. In the past, he had seen thousands of bears roaming in the winter, but this time only a few remained. Without hesitation, all the colors of the rainbow formed. It made a circle around the bears. Miraculously, snow flew in all the bears faces causing them to voyage into caves. Every bear had their own private cave. Suddenly, the bears eyes became heavy. Slowly all their eyes started to close. They slept through the whole winter. Incredibly, all the bears were saved that year causing the bear population to multiply. All the bears formed a line lifting Little Mirror up and sliding him down on the highest mountaintop in appreciation. The bears hibernate during the winter months because of the generosity of Little Mirror.

Birds fly north

Now the birds fly north in the winter. At one time, it was not the case, but Little Mirror helped them also. There were no worms for the birds to eat, because the grounds were frozen solid. There were no berries on the trees for the little birds to eat. They were pitiful. It was freezing that winter. The birds gathered together spreading their wings to keep each other warm. Their coats of feathers were not thick enough to withstand the freezing cold. The wind was whispering as the snow fell heavy on the trees. It was horrible. Little Mirror felt their hopelessness.

Less than a minute after seeing the vulnerable birds, Little Mirror sent his scouts out on a mission. The rainbow created a variety of colors and formed a line that guided the little birds to a warmer climate. The rainbow made a homemade arrow that speared through the sky warming all the birds as it guided them to a warmer climate, the south. Away, the birds flew, away to the warm climate of the south. After listening to chirping noises for hours, Little Mirror had to take actions.

There were so many creatures Little Mirror helped. One was the slow, slow, turtle. Have you personally wondered why the turtle has a hard shell? You know the turtle is one of the slowest animals. Being so slow, it was hard for turtles to escape form the larger animals. It needed protection, and fast. When danger appeared, the little turtles piled their bodies on top of each other to protect themselves from the predators, but the ones closest to the predators were killed instantly. It was terrible. One day, Little Mirror saw this firsthand. Thinking about his own back, Little Mirror created a shell made of walnuts and tree barks. The rainbow circled around the shell making it hard. Every turtle had its own private one. Now, they could hide when predators came within reach. Inside they stuck their head. Oh my, inside their shells was so comfortable. Now, the little turtles had their own home located on their backs.

The Dog

Little Mirror was growing up fast; he was experiencing puberty. He was now venturing out on his own and going deeper into the forest, away from the watchful eyes of momma and papa Ray. During this time, he encountered the Little Pup. Well, here's the story!

Centuries ago, dogs roamed the woods correlating with the strongest animals of all, the bears. These two roamed the countryside killing their preys mercilessly. Then one day, a little pup wandered near an old farmhouse. In the house, there lived a family of four, consisting of a mother, father, son and daughter. The father had made a homemade ball for the children to play with. While playing one day, the little boy threw the ball high in the sky. It landed near the feet of the little pup. Not being used to children, the little pup jumped up to attack the little boy. The pup was only used to killing, because it roamed the woods with the bears killing their victims with a vengeance. That's just the way the little pup was taught. Even young, the pup's bite was deadly enough to kill.

Little Mirror saw this out the corner of his eyes. He caused the colors of the rainbow to spin around and around. It reversed time. As time stood still, the little boy picked up the little dog and started stroking his fur. He rubbed and rubbed. My, it felt good to the little pup. It was the best feeling that the little pup had ever encountered. After that pleasant encounter, the pup visited the farmhouse every day. The children developed a bond with the little pup. From sunset to dawn the children played, throwing the ball. The little pup always retrieved it.

Then the little pup stopped coming. Years passed, and there was no pup.

Now, the little boy had become a man; he went into the forest to explore its magnificent sight. He saw the beautiful waterfalls, the colorful fish and the vegetation of the sea. Looking up in the trees, he saw the wild grapes hanging on the vines with an assortment of flowers everywhere. Unexpectedly, a huge bear got whiff of his scent and came charging out of nowhere. Before the man could *bat an eye*, a giant dog emerged and he tackled the bear, biting the bear with his large teeth. After battling the dog for hours, the bear backed off. He was shocked because the dog was his cohort, not his enemy. "Why?" he asked the dog. "I'm tired of being a bully. Look around bear," the dog continued to say. "No other animals like us. I want to be loved," the dog unremittingly said. "You made a bad choice," the bear said. "I'll sneak up on you when you are sleeping and destroy you! Now, aint that a coward. I will fight you as if you were a stranger the next time we meet." He hopped on one leg and tried to nurse his bad leg, while he retreated in the forest, leaving the man and the dog. "Gonna get you one day my ex-friend!" The dog shook his head. Because that's was the only way the bear could beat the dog. Why the bear didn't get it was beyond his reasoning.

Looking closer at the dog, the man realized it was the little pup that had become his friend years ago. He raced to hug the dog. From that day forward, they never parted from each other's sight. That's where the saying, **"a dog is a man's best friend"** came from.

The Little Pup

The Skunk

Do you know how the skunk got its smell? Well, the skunk didn't always have a bad odor, oh no. Living in the wild, the skunk's odor was so refreshing. He smelled like roses and lilies of the field. He attracted followers every place he went. Poor skunk, he had little time to mate or search for food. Even his enemies hunted the little skunk for its fragrance. There were only a few skunks. The skunk loathed its scent. He wanted a scent that would repel his enemy and protect him from his predators. He hated being the center of attention. Crying one day, he yelled out loud, "Who will help me? My scent is too refreshing. It attracts my predator." Little Mirror heard the skunk's heartfelt cry, and it touched his heart. Sending several rainbows out on a mission to find the foul odor, Little Mirror created an odor that would repel anything within a mile radius. It was a mixture of moss ball, raccoon musk and ant dusk. The odor was nauseating. Now, the little skunk could go anywhere without other predators coming within his reach. When the skunk raised his tail, all the other animals ran.

This proud skunk strutted around the forest proud he was no longer at the mercy of other animals.

The Monkey

Little Mirror always ventured out when his parents were napping, after all, that's what you do when you are experiencing growing pains. But he couldn't understand why momma monkey left her little ones at the mercy of the other animals, he was about to put a stop to this!

When you think of the monkey, what do you think of? Yes, a fun-loving creature that makes you laugh. Everyone knows the monkey has an energetic and explosive personality.

Well, centuries ago, this creature lacked parental skill. Momma monkey would leave her little ones for days to fend for themselves. These little ones depended solely on the generosity of the other animals in the forest. The birds and the rabbits were usually the ones who looked out for the monkey's little ones.

Momma Monkey, pacing back and forth, said, "When is the elephant coming? I have been waiting for hours."

The elephant marched along carefree like she didn't have a worry in the forest.

"Are you ready?" asked the Elephant.

Momma Monkey replied, "Yes."

"Who's watching over your little ones?" asked the elephant.

"I have no time to think about that," said momma monkey.

Little Mirror was identical to momma monkey, but he had the word Burden written on his forehead.

Little Mirror shakes his head. He is ready to whip Momma monkey with all the colors of the rainbow, but he waits.

Momma monkey hops on the elephant's back and along they go.

When they arrived at the rainforest, the two went on an eating spree, tasting all the exotic fruits in the forest.

Momma monkey and the elephant were the best of friends, but the elephant didn't like to take a bath. A stinky aroma followed the elephant everywhere she went. All the other animals were afraid to tell the elephant she stinks because this animal didn't play, especially when she got mad.

While the monkey was eating, the elephant farts right in the monkey's face, and started laughing.

"Ha, ha."

"Ooooooooooooooooo, you are so nasty; just lift me up elephant! Why you gotta do that any way? You are so nasty."

Momma monkey and the elephant lost tract of time. They were gone for days.

Then one day out of the blue, momma monkey said, "Take me home elephant. I got to check on the little ones."

"But monkey, let's go back to the rainforest first," said the elephant.

"Okay," said momma monkey, "The birds and rabbit will look after my little ones. Plus, that no count husband of mines done ran off with another family. I gotta have a little me time; what you think?"

"That's right sister girl," said the elephant.

They stayed another week gossiping with the other animals.

"What do you have for me today rabbit?" asked momma monkey.

"I have a little something, something," said the rabbit.

After eating and chatting for another week, momma monkey thanked the rabbit for her hospitality.

"Time to go. I got to check on the little ones," said momma monkey.

"Are you ready elephant?"

"Yes, my dear friend."

The elephant lowered its trunk and gave off a big fart. This time the odor knocked the birds out of the trees. Momma monkey frowned as she jumped on the elephant's back. "If you weren't my friend, I wouldn't talk to you because you are sooooooooooooooooo disgusting."

"Okay, girlies," the elephant said, "You know I gotta do what I gotta do."

Momma monkey started singing, "I'm home," as she circled the path leading to her home.

But wait, momma monkey saw a disturbing sight. She dropped the delights she was carrying in her mouth.

In plain sight, there was a leopard, and in his mouth was one of her little ones.

Ms. Squirrel grabbed her little ones after giving a disproving signal to momma monkey. The birds dropped their food and flew high up in the sky. The slow turtle said, "It's time to go," as he *eased on down the road*. All the other animals gave off a moaning sound. The hyena was no joke. She started pointing her finger at momma monkey and laughing with that nervous laugh, "Heeeeeeeeeeeeeeeeeeeeeeeeeeeeee, you've done it this time! you no count for nothing monkey. Now heeeeeeeeeeeeeeeeeeeee, gonna eat your baby!'' She laughed so hard her tongue got caught up in her throat, it almost choked her to death.

"What have I done?" said momma monkey.

Little Mirror takes all the colors of the rainbow and makes a belt. He hits momma monkey several times. Several colors of the rainbow were mad, especially yellow and blue. Little Mirror twisted several rainbows together and hit momma monkey several more times, one on the nose and another on the back. He continued until the colors of the rainbow felt some sort of pity for momma monkey and begged Little Mirror to stop.

Momma monkey started yelling, "Ouch, ouch, what's that?"

Little Mirror also shot a bolt straight towards the elephant. It hit her straight in the rear end.

 "Ouch, ouch," cried the elephant, "Why you hit me? I didn't do anything."

"Did you try to counsel your friend?" asked Little Mirror. "NOOOOOOOOOOOOOOOOOO," said the Elephant.

 "Well, you need to take ownership also. Now go!" said Little Mirror.

 Little Mirror frowned. "This creature needs a bath." Why didn't the other animals tell the elephant about his odor anyway?

 Little Mirror turned his attention to the leopard, "Oh you think you have a meal? Ha, ha, we will see."

Little Mirror loaded up all the colors of the rainbow and shot one rainbow right after another at the nasty leopard. The rainbow cornered the leopard. He saw all the colors of the rainbow coming straight towards him with a bolt of lightning riding the rainbow's back. The leopard was frightened out of his wits. He screamed. This acrobatic cat leaped high in the air. The leopard dropped the little monkey as he gracefully leaped up high in the sky.

 The leopard jumped so high that it touched the clouds with its claws and caused a rip and a heavy thunderstorm with winds blowing up to 100 miles an hour.

After falling back down from the sky, the leopard ran. He was afraid.

 Momma monkey jumped off the elephant's back.

The elephant ran while letting out another big gigantic fart and sneezed. She had been holding it for a long time. Plus, after seeing this sight, she had to cut a stink.

 The elephant ran fast. She didn't look back, because she didn't want Little Mirror to whip her behind.

"No more rides for you monkey," said the elephant. "You need to be more responsible."

Little Mirror shook his head. The elephant could have told momma monkey this a long time ago.

Momma Monkey gathered all her young ones. She clutched them giving them all hugs and kisses.

This ordeal had frightened her for real this time. But looking down at her body, her small tail now was long, and her body was hairy all over. Now her tail could hold on to everything allowing her to go high up into the trees away from her predators. Wow, this was amazing!

"I will never leave you again," said momma monkey.

After that encounter, momma monkey never left her little ones again. She became a doting mother.

Such an adorable animal

The Ivory Dove Prince's Story

Little Mirror was reaching the milestone of his life, he was about to become an adult. Little Mirror had another test to complete before his mission on earth was finished. It was to restore order to the Ivory Dove Kingdom. So, let's get on with the Story!

In the Kingdom of the Ivory Dove everything sparkles with gold and marble

The main room is the Throne Morning Room. This room is spacious with gold colored carpet that circles around another room in which King Calvin and Queen Josephine reside. The King sits in his royal robe in the highest chair, while Queen Josephine sits in a lower chair on his left side. Muscle bound guardians wearing masks flanked the King and Queen on both sides, while wielding their weapons ready to fight. King Calvin summons his son, Prince Michael, who comes in front of him and kneels before his father.

The stern looks the beautiful queen gave, people knew that she was the one who wore the pants, not by her words, but her haughty demeanor.

Prince Michael has a darker complexion. This alone was a sign of royalty. The maidens in the castle loved this chocolate delight, because in the kingdom of the Ivory Dove children born from royalty were different colors. This was a sign of purity.

"Prince Michael, do you know why I summoned you from your sword practice?" asked the king.

"No!" said Prince Michael. "Well, your mother is concerned because your twenty first birth-day is near, and you have yet to even show interest in a wife."

Prince Michael sucks his teeth and shakes his head. "But father, it is not I who have no interest in a wife. It's just that no maiden within our kingdom is willing to face the dragon that breathes fire from his heart and blows icicles from his nose. Why, my lord? Every princess thou have chosen has been killed by the dragon on the rooftop that breathes fire from its heart."

"You fool, thou must choose a princess that has strength as well as beauty. I have no pity for weakness," said Queen Josephine. "All I hear from you are excuses, excuses. Go ahead, tell him what we've decided dear!"

King Calvin clears his throat and takes a deep breath. Reluctantly he speaks, "Your mother and I have concluded that it's best for you to, uh, for you to..."

 Queen Josephine smacks her lips and cuts the King off impatiently, "You have until your birthday to find a wife who will be able to defeat the dragon. If not, you will be banished from this kingdom."

There was a loud gasp by everyone present.

"You will not be allowed to disgrace this family. All the other princes have wed, and we attended the royal ceremonies, but we have yet to host our own."

"But dearest mother, I only have twenty days until my birthday. Thou time is surely to run out."

"I told you he's not fit to be your heir," said Queen Josephine.

The king bows his head and leaves the main quarter. He goes into his favorite quarter. There King Calvin weeps openly.

  The Queen stares at the prince, secretly she hates him. "Go you fool! Your fate depends on you finding a princess willing to fight the dragon of the winter Ceiling," then she exits.

  Prince steps forward with pride, he lifts his chin up and walks away. Unbeknownst to the King's followers, Queen Josephine ran the palace and all the countrymen and countrywomen that were subjects of the king. She gave the orders in the privacy of their quarters. Even the prince wasn't aware of this.

But ssshhhhhhhhhhhh, this was Queen Josephine's little secret. Later, King Calvin and Prince Michael will discover more secrets about Queen Josephine.

The prince goes to his stable where his prize procession, his horse, Blazing Lightning is grazing. He saddled him up and galloped off into the forest. He rides it seemed like for hours.

Prince jumps off his horse and sits under a tree.

Prince Michael drifted into a deep sleep. While sleeping, he was playing with his trusted friend, guard-man, Waymond and Kelvin. They both had grew up with the prince until the queen banished them from the Ivory Tower Kingdom. Waymond was one of the best knights of the Ivory Dove palace, but Queen Josephine hated Waymond. She hated everyone that loved Prince Michael.

Waymond and Prince Michael did everything together. They fought enemies of the Ivory Dove Tower and were victors. They chased the maidens of the Ivory Dove Tower and princesses together wooing the fair maidens, until King Calvin put a stop to this foolishness.

Waymond was Prince Michael's brother not by blood, but by love.

Queen Josephine plotted to do away with them, because they cut up and laughed all the time. The queen hated laughter. She wanted complete silence when she entered the room. This was crazy.

One day, the queen went outside unto the Gold Rush Banquet Hall. She was mad at the King. Everyone was laughing and enjoying Prince Michael's friend Kelvin, who was performing. The queen had two personalities that she kept hidden. The queen always thought someone was laughing at her. "Stop this nonsense," she said while she entered the room. Everyone outside was astonished. Prince Michael was laughing with his two trusted friends, the joker, Kelvin and Waymond.

Waymond had earned his honors and respect by defeating all of King Calvin's adversaries. Kelvin lit up the palace with his jokes. King Calvin truly loved him. Kelvin tried to make the Queen laugh, but Queen Josephine got even madder.

"Go!" the queen ordered Waymond and Kelvin. "You are now banished from the Ivory Tower Kingdom." Half the guardsmen moved toward Prince Michael and Waymond's sides. The sides had been drawn and they were ready to battle. The humpback eagle came flying toward the Prince. This animal protected the prince, especially when he got into trouble. She was ready to fight, and boy this bird was mad. The guardsmen on the side of the queen looked afraid, because Prince Michael and Black Knight, Waymond were forces that couldn't be beat.

King Calvin stepped forward. The prince loved his father and would never disrespect him, even though he knew his father was under the spell of his queen, his mother. The Prince bowed his head showing respect for his father. The queen continued to say, "I told Kelvin and Waymond they're banished." "Well," said the king, "It is so. They are banished to the land of the Smelly Springs." You will be fed daily, but the odor from the creatures will cause you to repel food. Thus, you both will perish.

The queen stepped forward. "Ha, ha, this will teach you to not laugh at your queen again, you fool."

"But mother," Prince Michael said, "they are my trusted companions." "You weakling," Queen Josephine replied, "get a backbone!" She strutted off. "Guards take the prisoners away."

The prince looked at his father. The king raised his hands. This meant the order must be carried out.

Prince Michael and Waymond could have disobeyed the King because no one, I mean no one, had come close to beating Prince Michael and his trusted companion, Waymond, not even King Calvin when they had swordsmen practice. Plus, Prince Michael had battled the best and he was victorious every single time. The prince signaled, for his guards to retreat. He loved his father that much, even though he was losing respect for him with every passing day.

Prince Michael looked at the King, but the king looked away.

"Okay father, we will honor your wishes," said Prince Michael.

"My son, the Queen has her reasons, but she is my queen." Then King Calvin ordered the guards to take the prince's two trusted friends to the land of the Smelly Springs. The prince walked off, dropping his head. What will he tell Kelvin and Waymond's parents?

The prince loved Kelvin like a brother, this jokester was so filled with laughter. Every time Kelvin entered the palace, people surrounded him. It was different with his companion Waymond. The prince wondered how he was going to continue without him, because Waymond knew all his secrets. They had grown up together. Waymond's parents were the prince's caretakers. Waymond knew all the prince's secrets. One of them had caused him so much pain, because the prince thought the queen hated him. Plus, the prince and Waymond had chased after maidens together.

Waymond always made him smile. But even this, Prince Michael couldn't understand why the Queen lacked compassion for even him. It was too much for him to explain away.

The Prince had dozed off for only a couple of minutes, but the plights of his two best friends were fresh on his mind. Will he ever see them again? He wondered.

"Enough of that, I need to find Little Mirror!"

Prince Michael had heard stories about Little Mirror, and he needed his help. So, he jumped back on Blazing Lightning, because he had to find this humble creature that could lift burdens and place it on his own back.

Little Mirror was resting by his favorite spot, the Goldfish Lake. Prince Michael greeted Little Mirror before he proceeded to tell Little Mirror about his plight.

"Oh, little mirror," the prince said. 'I am in a dreadful dilemma. I must find a suitable princess that my parents will appreciate and approve. She must be beautiful enough to hold them speechless for an hour. She must be humble enough to wash the king and queen's feet, and powerful enough to defeat the dragon that lives on the rooftop above the palace who breaths fire from its heart and blows icicles from its nose. If the princess fails, she will be fed to the creatures of the lake!"

The prince cried. "How can I find such a princess?"

The task seemed impossible to the prince, because it seemed so hopeless. But to Little Mirror, it was like swimming in the lake. Little Mirror felt the prince's pain and sorrow. He thought about how he could help the prince, because he knew of a princess that had all these characteristics and more. She too had once come to him for help.

Little mirror, sitting now close by Prince Michael, is identical to the prince but with one exception. He has the word burden written on his forehead. Little Mirror gets ready, and he loads up his rainbows.

"Why is such a handsome prince looking so lost?" asked Little Mirror.

"This task thou father and mother besieged me to do, it's not within my power."

"Thou undertakings are mine, don't let one task weigh you down Prince Michael," said Little Mirror.

The rainbow came from Little Mirror's back and wrapped around the prince until he was completely covered in colors. Once it started to unwrap, the prince was no longer there. He had been transported to an unknown land.

The prince rubbed his eyes. High on top of a high mountain, the prince saw a castle. This castle was grand. It was called the Palace of the Rose Garden, and as he drew near, he saw a king and queen. They both were gathered around the center of the Rose Palace Gates surrounding the main entry of the palace. The palace was grander than you could ever imagine. It had toasted melon, with strawberries sandwiched between pickles, and spices stationed on the rooftop. Little what nots were sprinkled with spices on top of delicacies of fruits.

Small maidens were lined up by the roses while singing a relaxing song.

Prince Michael got off Blazing Lightning and let his horse graze in the meadows while he approached the rose maiden and rose men.

"Where is the main quarter?" asked the prince.

Maiden looks up, "Thou prince, there is a bridge near the rose garden that is filled with creatures of all sorts. Go swiftly, the sea creature dines on aliens. Look past the hanging trees with all sorts of fruits, there you will find a vineyard draping a stairway. Behind the rose bushes, there is a door leading to the castle."

"But wait," said the rose maid, "I will show you the way." She gazed at Prince Michael, because she had never seen anyone so stunning.

The prince trudged on to find a princess willing to fight the dragon on top of the palace.

The palace was spectacular with gardens of all colored roses covering every inch and crack. On the grounds of the palace there were spectacular waterfalls. Everyone was beautiful in their own rights.

When the prince and maiden reached the palace, the prince was speechless. This place was equal to the Ivory Dove in its magnificent beauty. All the quarters in the palace were covered with jewels.

Prince Michael was awestruck.

Little Mirror was standing beside the king posing as one of the guards. He had several bolts of lightning rods in both hands, because he was ready to battle. Roses were scattered beside his feet.

Prince Michael entered the room. There facing him was King Larry, the Rose King, and on the opposite side was a beauty that seemed unreal, his queen, Queen Free. The queen's eyes had a pink diamond in the middle, her skin was Ivory, and she had flowing black lots. The queen's beauty mesmerized Prince Michael; time paused.

"Draw closer my son," said King Larry. "What brings you to the Palace of the Rose Tower?"

"My Lord, I'm a noble prince, but my cause is not noble."

The King Larry beckoned the prince to come closer, "Thou have something thou want to ask the Rose King?"

"Yes, my Lord," said the prince.

"Speak!" said the King.

"I journey from a far-off land, searching for a princess that has power and wit. She must be clever, clever enough to undertake a daunting task of defeating a notorious nuisance, the dragon of the Heart. This nuisance devours everything in its sight." The prince continued "The princess must be beautiful, courageous and humble. If she doesn't defeat the dragon of the heart, she will perish in the winter lake. If she succeeds, the princess will become my wife."

The King is shocked by the prince's request, and he drops his scepter. His face has a bewildered look on it.

The King Larry draws his sword. "You will perish for this," said King Larry.

Prince Michael pulls out his sword, and the battle began. Both the prince and the king were excellent swordsmen. They fought and fought until Little Mirror stopped them.

"You fool," said the Queen. "This will be the end of you, but before you perish, my Lord, summon Princess Tammy."

Princess Tammy walks in slowly. She is draping in exquisite beauty. She bows her head before her father, King Larry. If you think of beauty, this goes beyond the physical façade, oh, yes! She was "a gift to the eyes." Princess Tammy embodied light. She had busy curls that fell to her feet. She had a statuette figure.

The prince was lost in the princess' beauty for an hour. After regaining consciousness, the prince continued his story about how there had been many princesses that had failed to defeat the dragon, and all had perished in the winter lake.

The king standing up, "Slay him, Slay Him! Thou will be punished for asking the Rose Garden king such an absurd thing." King Larry loved his daughter. He taught her everything she needed to know to protect the Rose palace. After all, she battled his most trusted knights, the knights of "the Round Table."

"Slay him!" the king said again. "But before you do, take him to Flowery Lake where the Rose monster lives. This creature will surely devour him without you using your sword."

What about the Queen?

The queen had a weird look on her face, but my goodness she was beautiful also.

"Stand UP!" said the queen. "Now thou shall soon see the fury of the king."

Little mirror standing nearby ran forward saying, "It is what it needs to be."

He grabs his holster filled with rainbows and pulls out one bolt of lightning and aims it straight toward the king. It hits the king knocking him of his throne. The colors of the rainbow encircled the king and queen causing a smoke to engulf the whole palace. Bright colors lit up the palace.

Then the smoke stops. What was going on? Now King Larry was smiling. He looked like he was in a euphoric state.

Little Mirror had to teach King Larry a lesson in humility, because at one time King Larry valued his possessions more than the subjects he represented. This was a no no for Little Mirror! And would you believe it, he was unfaithful to Queen Free until Little Mirror stopped him from making a fool out of himself at his age.

King Larry beckoned his knights to release the prince.

"Go!" said King Larry. "May petals of roses light your heart as you continue your journey."

Prince Michael struts toward the princess while not looking directly at her, because he didn't want to be swept away by her beauty. He swept the princess up and put a bag on her head. He had no time to waste, on to the Ivory Tower. It was two days before his twenty-first birthday.

Unbeknownst to the prince, his wicked mother, the Queen, had sent out her guardsmen to prevent him from returning. But Little Mirror had confused them, so they went trailing a wild goose chase. In other words, the wrong way.

Prince Michael knew his journey wasn't going to be easy, but he had his sword ready.

After traveling for an hour, Prince Michael approached a strange looking lake. It was the lake where Smelly Feet's lived. He had heard stories about how Smelly Feet trapped all the princes in the lake so she could just gaze into their eyes until they weren't anymore. Their remains left a foul odor. Prince Michael also wandered what happened to his two friends, Waymond, the knight and Kelvin, the mischief-maker. But his thoughts were interrupted by a weird sound. When the prince got closer, he smelled a foul odor. It smelled so repugnant that he started gasping for his breath. By then, the little princess was asleep. Then out of nowhere, a swarm of flies surrounded him. He tried to dodge them, but these creatures cornered him. The prince tried to hide behind a big rock, but the creatures swarmed around him. The smell was bad. The prince gave out a loud cry because he couldn't see. Then he heard another strange sound. Smelly Feet had woken up, and she was mad. She tried to jump on top of him with one of her legs while the other two knocked him around and around. This creature had a vulgar odor, and the scent was driving Prince Michael crazy. They struggled and struggled. Smelly Feet started smiling because she could taste victory, but the prince was determined that this creature would not get the best of him. They fought and fought until the princess woke up, "What's that?" asked Smelly Feet. The Princess took the bag off her head to check out the bad smell and the noise. Smelly Feet looked at the princess and was spellbound; She couldn't move causing her to lose her hold on Prince Michael. Prince Michael rolled around on the ground still gasping for air.

While rolling down the hill, Prince Michael heard noises by the edge of the cage. He drew his sword prepared to fight because he didn't play. Either you were against him or for him. Either he would win or lose, a third option wasn't possible. The closer he got, the more the noise sounded familiar. When he got closer, the prince noticed that something about the voice seemed so familiar. It sounded like his friend, Kelvin.

When the prince inspected the cage, he saw an awful sight. Kelvin was covered with hair all over his skinny body and behind him looking even more weird was Waymond. Waymond had a hopeless look on his face. But when the two saw the prince, they both gave out two weird sounds from their mouths. The prince released Kelvin first, because he was tied to seaweed to the point that he couldn't move. Kelvin's face had a hopeless look on it. The prince then focused his attention on Waymond. Waymond just stared into an empty space because he was so used to starting at that awful sight Smelly Feet. He couldn't look anyone in their eyes.

The prince gathered them both up and stationed them on his horse before Smelly Feet woke up. "Go Lightning Speed take them to the Land of the Ivory Tower."

"Go, Lightning Speed, go to the palace and get Kelly," said Prince Michael. **"Kelly will know what to do."**

Lightning speeded off. Lightning Speed noodled, and with lightning speed, he trotted on.

The journey back to the Ivory tower wasn't easy. The prince had to fight several more times before he reached the Ivory Dove Palace. But he was victorious. After all, his father was the best swordsmen in the kingdom, but King Calvin stopped practicing after the Queen complained about this little pastime.

Prince Michael pitied the King. On so many occasions he asked his father why he didn't just stand up to his mother, the Queen. His father just walked away. King Calvin was blinded by Queen Josephine's beauty.

Prince Michael finally arrived at the Kingdom of the Ivory Dove Palace.

The prince escorted the princess to the main halls, where King Calvin and Queen Josephine were sitting.

When Queen Josephine gets a glimpse of the Prince, she drops her scepter. Her face looked like she had seen a ghost, because she was so hopeful that the prince would be slayed. She secretly wanted the Prince dead, later you will find out why.

"Cometh here my son," said the King. He embraces the prince.

Little Mirror smiled disguised as the king's trusted swordsman.

"Father, I traveled a long distance, but I found a princess willing to fight the dragon of the heart."

He takes the bag off the princess' head. The queen and king were mesmerized by the princess' beauty for an hour. The princess was the most exquisite being they had ever seen. The queen had never seen anyone equivalent to the beauty she possessed. This made her more enraged.

"My Lord, this is the princess of the Rose garden. She possesses all the qualities that you wanted. She is humble, beautiful and strong. She will defeat the dragon of the heart."

The Rose princess stepped forward, she gets a pail of water and started washing the king and queen's feet.

"What can this princess do? She's too frail to fight the dragon of the heart."

"That may be true my lady, but don't be fooled by my exquisite looks. My father trained me as a knight to protect the Rose palace. He trained me from the best of the best, the knights of the Round Table."

"Thou word you spoken, only tells me you're a liar!"

"Your mother only wants the best princess for you, my son. So be gone. The princess's fate depends on her defeating the creature that laughs at maidens, devouring them like they are flies. If she defeats this nuisance, she will be worthy of you, my son."

The king and queen leaves, but the king branches off in another direction. He goes in his private living space where he weeps.

"I'm tired, tired of my queen but I love her. This love I have for her prevents me from doing away with her. This evilness by the Queen can't continue but what can I do? I'm so lost."

Little Mirror tells the prince, "It's time my Lord, time for you to see what needs to be."

"Come here, Prince Michael. I will tell you and Princess Tammy how you can defeat the dragon of the heart. Just think my dear princess, think of hot and cold. If something is too hot, it needs to be cooled off. Well, the dragon will heat you up first, then later he will try to freeze you." Little Mirror goes on to tell the princess, how to defeat the dragon.

Little Mirror is identical to the Prince, but on his forehead, is the word burden. Little Mirror goes on to say this, "Before you go to the rooftop, think about all the love you have inside. Think about the love you feel for the prince. Just know when there is love, there is light. Walk backward when you get close to the doorway. Turn around and step to the left of the dragon. This is the dragon's blind spot. He will gaze at you with his ice-cold eyes. Use your sword as a shield to blind him. He will roll over and breathe fire from his heart. Gaze steadily at the fire. Don't move. The fire will form a circle enclosing you inward, but your loving heart, princess, will cool the flames. Then the dragon will cause icicles to come out of his nose causing a blizzard. Wave the sword pointing it to the south and back up. He will shoot more icicles forward. Back up and hit the icicles behind your back. Cough three times and turn your back to the left, then back facing the beast. All the fire that he has inside of him will surge forward. Gaze at it but still fight the beast with all your strength. His heart will become weak, because with every fireball and icicle it weakens his heart. The dragon will attempt to retrieve your heart, but the love you had inside your heart will repel the creature and cause him to retrieve his claws swiftly."

"Now my child, you must fight, fight will all your might. Fight for your prince. Fight for honor and fight for the right of the unforgotten. This fighting spirit will save you my princess."

The princess did all that Little Mirror told her to do.

The dragon and the princess fought and fought. The palace shook. The whole countryside was shaking causing earthquakes. The people were afraid, and they went into hiding.

"Ha, ha," said the dragon mocking the princess. "You are tough, but you are not equal to me. I have cold, I have hot on my side. Give up princess!"

"Ohhhhhhhhhhhhhhhhhhh no," replied the princess. "Hot and cold don't bother me. It only makes me madder."

The dragon's heart got bigger in his chest. "Oh, look at me," said the dragon. "Now, it's about to get bad." The dragon begins to fight with all his might. The dragon's heart was beating faster and faster. Then, slower and slower. "OOOOOOOOOOOOOOOOO, what is happening to me? I feel warm." The dragon reached out to get the princess's heart but was repelled by the love inside her heart.

A transformation was occurring before the princess' eyes. A light burst forward, blinding the princess.

Finally, there was no light and standing in its place was a beauty that embodied loveliness. A beauty that matched the queen. She was identical to the queen, but she displayed elegance and grace. There seemed to be a glow around her, this was invisible to the naked eye.

This beautiful exquisite creature gave details to how the fake queen was her sister that had misled her years ago and tried to throw her into winter lake because she was jealous of her. Even though the real queen and the maiden were identical in beauty, the real queen symbolized all the things that the false queen was not such as happy, humble and patient.

Then an amazing thing happened. Out of the lake, heat elevated high in the sky. There emerged a fair maiden, whose beauty was so majestic that it caused both the princess and the real queen to pause for an hour. But wait, the maiden in the lake was the real queen's daughter. The real queen was pregnant when she was left on the rooftop. The real queen gave birth before she was transformed into a dragon. Another twist, the queen's daughter was ivory unlike her parents, who were dark brown. Little Mirror did this to show that beauty comes in all colors.

The real queen, the Ivory Dove Princess, and the real queen's daughter hugged and walked down from the rooftop.

The prince is waiting by the stairway. When the prince sees all the exquisite beauties, he is mesmerized; it seemed like it was an eternity for the prince. But the three beauties waited until Little Mirror signaled them to come closer. Little Mirror tells the young princess to wait until her real mother confronts the King and tells her story.

 The prince escorted the princess and the real queen to the main quarters.

"What's this?" the king asked, but then he was spellbound for two hours.

The Queen on the other hand shouted, "What's this?" "This is plain evilness!" she yelled. Then she was spell bound for three hours.

 The real queen stepped forward and begins to tell her story.

"One day, unexpectedly, I was summoned to the Wall room. There dressed as a maiden in fair clothing with her face covered in a blue velvet veil, but I knew who she was, she was my evil twin sister, Mary Jo. She asked to speak to me, so I told her to follow me on top of the roof. King Calvin didn't know I had a twin sister, because I wanted to protect him from my evil twin. My evil twin destroyed everyone that met her, and she sucked the life out of the people whom loved her the most. That's why I never told King Calvin about her presence. After a lengthy talk on the rooftop, what happened next was just plain evil. My wicked sister pushed me off the roof into the lake of fire that was used to burn animals that had wandered into the garden of the palace. The fire didn't want to harm me, so it circled my body and placed me on the rooftop, where I eventually became a dragon."

"Stop, she is evil, slay her!" said the wicked queen.

The King Calvin and Prince Michael did a double take, as they looked at each other. The King thinking out Loud, "Yes, it is odd all my troubles seemed to begin right after that visit from the fair maiden." The king said out loud, "But if it hadn't been for Little Mirror, my burdens would have destroyed me. Now that I think about it, I was happier before the maiden came to the palace. Yes, it was right after the queen went on the rooftop and spoke secretly with the maiden. After that, Queen Josephine's whole demeanor changed. Oh my, when she came down, she was so different. OHHHHHHHHHHHHHH, she seemed to hate everything. Why she didn't even want the prince around her anymore. I had to get a nurse maiden to look after him, because she hated prince Michael."

"Yes," said the prince. "After mother came down from the rooftop, she wasn't the same. She no longer wanted me around her."

Little Mirror ran forward releasing all the colors of the rainbows. The rainbows circled around both the real queen and the evil queen.

Little Mirror selected bright rainbows, but instead of shooting them, he blew them on top of the real queen's head.

Now, the king's eyes became opened.

"Be gone from my sight," he said, pointing to the evil queen.

Guards escorted the fake queen up on the rooftop and were about to push her into the frozen zone. Little Mirror stopped them, because the real queen didn't want her sister to be destroyed. She still loved her. So, Little Mirror put the evil queen into a time suspension with the hope that one day she would make atonement for her evilness. Little Mirror did this at the request of Queen Josephine.

On the rooftop, suddenly there was a boom. Out from the lake emerged maiden, countrymen and animals of all sorts. Flowers came alive. Where there were bushes, now roses appeared again.

But wait, I forget to tell you what happen to Waymond and Kelvin, the prince's trusted friends.

Blazing Lightning took them to the Ivory Dove Tower, but before the horse entered the gates, he saw Kelly talking to several fair maidens. The horse noodles, and Kelly turned around. Kelly sees Waymond and Kelvin lying down on the horse. He excuses himself and rushes to their aid. Kelly knows for Blazing Lightning to return without Prince Michael it must be bad. Nevertheless, he had to take these two home and fast.

Now let's get back to Waymond and kelvin!

After years of living in the lake with Smelly Feet, Waymond couldn't speak. Waymond secretly had fallen in love with Smelly Feet. After several years of staring at her, he began to see her good qualities. Even Smelly Feet was saddened by Waymond's departure. When Waymond left, she became heartbroken because she loved him.

Let's get back to all the transformation that were happening at the Ivory Dove Palace. When all the burdens throughout the Ivory Dove were lifted, Smelly Feet was transformed back into a rightful heir, a princess. She was so beautiful that the lake that she resided in turned into the most magnificent lake with flowers and greenery that ever graced the earth.

Now it was her mission to find Waymond, her love. After weeks of searching, her guards led her to an old cottage where Waymond's humble parents resided.

The princess was surrounded by guards. She was so beautiful that her guardsmen had to wear a mask to shield her beauty.

Entering the cottage, the princess noticed how humble it looked. One guard moved forward and said, "Greetings, Princess Teresa is looking for your son Waymond." His parents motioned her to come closer.

"Why are you looking for Waymond?" the mother asked. Then the father said, "Waymond hasn't spoken since he came home from the Lake of Smelly Feet."

"Summon him," said Princess Teresa.

"Okay my fair lady," said Waymond's parents. "We will fetch him." Waymond came walking, slumped over. The princess spoke, but he kept looking down. "I've heard that voice before," said Waymond. "But where?"

Then Princess Teresa lifted Waymond's head. "It is me, Smelly Feet." Waymond backed back. "How and why?"

Princess Teresa proceeded to tell Waymond about how the wicked queen had showed up at her kingdom pretending that she wanted to find a princess for her son, but she lied because she had heard about the princess' fighting skills and her beauty. This had enraged the queen of the Ivory Tower, because she was jealous of anyone that displayed genuine beauty that came from the heart.

 The wicked queen had to do something, and fast. She enlisted two of her trusted guards, and they went in search of Princess Teresa, the princess that embraced all the children in her kingdom making sure their needs were met. The evil queen lowered the princess to the lake called Smelly Feet. The smell was suffocating. There Princess Teresa was forced to live in the lake. The princess ate rotten food until she changed into an unrecognizable creature. Waymond yelled. Little Mirror, standing beside Waymond identical to him, caused his rainbows to swish around Waymond. This caused Waymond's demeanor to change back into a strong looking guardsman. His parents looked at each other and shouted because after Lightning Speed brought him home, Waymond basically was helpless. He had to be cared for by his parents. The princess hugged and kissed Waymond. "Now, before we go back to my kingdom, you must be ordained and accept your rightful title, a Prince," said Princess Teresa.

    Princess Teresa went on to tell Waymond how his mother was dying, and that's why she gave him up to her brother, the king of Ivory Tower, when Waymond was only a babe. The king assigned a nobleman and his wife to raise Waymond. In time, his surrogate parents grew to love him like he was their child. At the Ivory Dove palace, he was raised as a guardsman, eventually becoming a knight to Prince Michael. Waymond still couldn't remember things, but when he came close to the palace, he started to remember everything. When the Princess and Waymond arrived, it seemed like everyone was expecting them. Prince Michel ran up and hugged him. "I missed you, my trusted friend."

 Waymond started to cry, but not because he was sad. It was because it had been so long since he seen his two beloved friends. "I missed you too, my friend," said Waymond. They hugged for hours before catching up on the affairs of the land.

But what happened to Kelvin the clown? When Lightning Speed arrived back to the palace Kelly, the maiden's man, and one of the best fighters in the Ivory Tower took Kelvin to the palace into the rainforest' room. There Kelvin stayed for several months. He bathed and bathed. The king knew something bad must have happened, so he let Kelvin stay in the room because he noticed Kelvin was no longer happy. Plus, Kelvin had a bad smell. The king had heard stories about the lake of Smelly Feet, that's why he gave Kelvin time. But secretly, King Calvin missed Kelvin's explosive personality. The king laughed and laughed thinking back of how awful Kelvin smelled when he arrived on the back of Lightning Speed. After months of rubbing, Kelvin had gotten rid of that awful smell, but he lacked the joy he once had.

King Calvin summoned Kelvin. Kelvin came. When he saw his friends, he ran and fell over the scepter. The king and Little Mirror fell out laughing. "Kelvin," Little Mirror said, "When are you gonna become a nobleman?"

The prince and princess spread the word of Little Mirror. People came from far and near to place their burdens on his back. He had adventures after adventures. This became Little Mirror's mission.

He traveled all over lifting burdens. The list went on and on, rats, squirrels, bears, frogs, dogs, and giraffes. Every creature under the sun, Little Mirror helped. Slowly but surely, Little Mirror's back got heavier and heavier. Little Mirror could barely move.

One day as little mirror was resting, Mamma Ray noticed a dramatic change in his appearance. Little Mirror wanted to see himself, so Mama Ray took him to a river so he could see his own reflection. There was a bulge in the front of Little Mirror, and when he touched it, it cracked causing him to roll forward. He landed in the raging river, swish, swish. Lightning, thunder, rain and hail showered as the elements reclaimed what were theirs.

Wham! Boom! Boom! The mirror shattered, and Little Mirror became a full circular being, producing more light than Momma and Papa Ray combined. He smiled as he climbed out of his frame, growing larger every second. All the stars, planets and clouds formed a circle to clothe him with a shine of honor. All the seasons flashed before his eyes; spring with its flowers budding; the summer heat, and winter snowstorms and fall with its designer leaves. Oh, it was a splendorous sight.

His eyes received every scrap of light as heaven and earth collided and circled back and forth. Finally, there was calmness over the whole earth. Little Mirror leaped forward as he embodied the light. As he circled the sky, he blew kisses of appreciation to his adopted parents.

So, if you are a child and are afraid to go to sleep, think about Little Mirror, the being that once thrived and lived within our reach. He lifted our burden from our hearts. He never murmured or complained about how heavy the load. The colors of the rainbow reflected the sorrows, and with a little dab of sugar he dipped all our troubles in the sky.

Little Mirror's parents loved him dearly. They saw the love he displayed for the earth. When our burdens become more than we can stand, when the world seems so overwhelming, Little Mirror will return to the earth disguised in yet another form.

Every year, flowers blossom with an assortment of colors of the rainbow to express Little Mirror's undying love. Pinch off a petal and you will see, because it is filled with love. He did it to serve as a reminder to be forgiving of yourself and help others. Lift their burdens, so when the time comes to lift yours, someone will be there for you.

How winter came about

Little Mirror, now the sun, reflected on his life on earth. One of his intricate tasks was when he created another season, winter. Even though he was the sun, his memories on earth were still precious to him.

Well, here's the story about how winter came about.

Long ago, there were only three seasons, spring, summer and fall. There was no winter. Sit back and let me tell you how winter came about.

In a ragged cottage, there lived a man whose life passion was to belittle people, because he lacked compassion. One reason why is he didn't have anyone to pattern his thoughts and behaviors from. You see, his parents died when he was a little babe. Now, Gorgeous' sole purpose in life was to demean others and make their lives a living nightmare. He lived far away in the forest, away from civilization on a steep hill surrounded by mountains. When he ventured out among people, he was rude and disgusting. He was shunned by most people.

But for the unsuspecting females who wanted to get to know him, it was a disaster. Gorgeous was stunning. Everything about him was perfect. Gorgeous had curly hair with brown diamond lenses in his eyes. This gave off a soothing effect like the river-falls flowing over the riverbanks. His statuesque built captured the essence of beauty. Women sought him out because of his breathtaking looks. But once the women got to know him, they fled for dear life because his tongue spurred out offensive language in their presence that even his beauty couldn't captivate them enough to stay.

But little did anyone know, Gorgeous loved being alone because his heart had become half ice. His face always looked blank, giving off a lifeless appearance. There was one beautiful lady, named Mary Jo, this lovely, curvy woman loved Gorgeous. She walked in the forest daily just to be close to him, but this selfish man didn't have any compassion. He *couldn't see the forest for the trees.* Mary Jo tried to reason with Gorgeous about if he continued treating everyone badly, one day he will be by himself with only regrets. One day Gorgeous went too far, he called Mary Jo the F. word. Mary Jo swirled her head around and said, "my momma didn't raise no fools." She strutted off, reclaiming her dignity that she had somehow lost years ago. But Gorgeous, laughed and continued to do what he did, complained.

 Finally, Mary Jo gave up. and left him alone. After all, that was what he wanted anyway.

   Mary Jo found herself a real man. He was her best friend's brother. Lady Shaw was her best friend. She was the type of person that treated everyone with admiration, not by words, but by her actions. Lady Shaw was a small petite woman but was a force of nature when someone offended someone she loved.

She had been trying for years to get Mary Jo to notice her brother, but Mary Jo being stubborn had her eyes only on Gorgeous.

   Now Gorgeous on the other hand, believed that no one could match up to his exquisiteness or his cleverness. Gloating over himself daily, he didn't let any woman get close to his perfection. Every spring, he dressed in light clothing and went into the woods. He pulled up berry bushes, vegetation and other food that he could find. He demolished everything that was edible. Why you ask? Because he felt that animals were not entitled to the free food that nature created. "Let then work for it," he would say. Little did he know that someone was watching him. It was Little Mirror.

   When it was time for fall, the leaves started falling on the ground. Gorgeous went into a frenzy because he hated this season with a passion. Why do the trees give up its leaves anyway he thought?

   The color of the leaves is so bright. "Ah," he said, "it's so disguising." He complained every day about little simple matters. Never did he do an act of kindness. Never did he speak a pleasant word, because all his thoughts were ice cold and the rage, he had inside had turned his semi-cold heart, completely to ice.

When spring came, you would think the aroma, the flowers blossoming, and the birds chirping would be wonderful. Oh no, he complained more. The noise caused him to feel trapped. The scent from the fragrance of flowers caused him to have anxiety attacks. He didn't like taking a bath so anything that smelled refreshing, irritated him.

"I hate the birds and their noisy sounds," he said. "If I see another bird, it will be stew time for sure."

After years of hearing this, Little Mirror did something unique. Instead of helping Gorgeous with the color of the rainbow, the color of the rainbow reversed after leaving his back. The rainbow returned within a few feet of its target destination. The breathtaking man that was once beautiful, was now a grumpy man and boy, he was old. He seemed to be erased from existence. It was like he never existed. But wait, the once handsome man, now looked white. His beard was snowflakes with icicles. His voice had a hoarse sound. "I'm calling you," Little Mirror said, "winter!" "You will be the hardest season of all. This will be your punishment, because of your lack of respect for others."

The first winter was icy-cold. The wind was harsh on the skin. People was shocked, because they only remembered having three seasons and this one just popped up out of nowhere. Oh, this season was no doubt the toughest of all. People had to gather wood, put on extra clothing, and stay in more because the chill of the snow prevented them from staying out too long. Ohoooooooooooooo, it was bad. A lot of animals died that year. "What is this?" Gorgeous said, once he saw his reflection in the river. He screamed, "My looks, my looks are gone!" "Yes!" said Little Mirror. "This is what your arrogances and haughtiness have caused you, your looks!" There Gorgeous stood an icy-pale creature, with long nails made of icicles. Hideous in appearance, his looks were gone with nothing to glorify his presence on earth. "It's good," said Little Mirror. "Now, you can only come out in the cold winter months.

Respect my wishes. Don't abuse your authority, because the consequences could have an undesirable effect on the environment."

At first, Winter, as he was now called, honored Little Mirror's wishes. Then he got haughty. "Why should I respect Little Mirror's wishes? What can he do to me that hasn't already been done?" Then he did the unthinkable, he came out in the summer, the fall and the spring. Ms. Spring was making her rounds above the trees and sprinkling dust on buds in the trees. When a windstorm came breezing by her, "Who are you?" she asked. "Ha, ha, I'm Mr. Winter, ha, ha. I can do as I please." He blew breezes of ice on the young buds in the adjourning trees. "Go!" Spring said, "it's not your time." "No!" Winter said, as he froze the buds in the adjourning tree. "It feels so good!" Shortly after, he left, but the damages were already done. All the fruit trees were destroyed that year.

Summer came with a vengeance, the heat was hot, hot. "I will put a stop to this," Mr. Winter said as sat on his throne. He scooped up his belongs and paid summer a visit. "Who are you?" asked Summer. "It's me," Mr. Winter said, "the ghastliest season of all." "Get away from here!" Summer shouted. "It is not your time." "Oh, Noooooooooooooooooooooo," she said as Mr. Winter gusted his icy finger. Mr. Winter, being a bully, pushed Summer out of the way and continued icing everything in sight. He put his cold gusty finger on Summer, causing her to lose her sting that year. Summer was mild. It was like it was Spring instead of Summer. This caused several eruptions in the atmosphere. Consequently, most of the crops were destroyed that year also. The trees didn't know what to do. "How could this happen," thought Little Mirror. But then, winter was about to tackle fall, fall was making her rounds when winter sneaked up on her, but fall wasn't having it. "You might bully the other seasons but, you better not mess with me!" She pointed her fingers and all the leaves danced in place; they were ready to battle. "Go head" yelled winter, 'I don't need this." This character is causing too much trouble everywhere. "I'll fix this," Little Mirror said as the rainbow circled around Mr. Winter. Suddenly, flabbergasted, Little Mirror couldn't believe his eyes. Winter's whole demeanor changed. He became obedient from that point on. Mr. Winter's whole outlook on life changed. He now embraced the other seasons. He even helped some of the smaller creatures find shelters in the cold winter months. In appreciation, Little Mirror gave him a whole region of his own, the North Pole, a place that stayed Winter year-round. Little Mirror also designed an area where the rose princes once lived. This also remained winter year-round.

Now, let's go back to what happened to Prince Michael, Waymond, the Knight but now a prince, and Kelvin, the clown. After the three united, they had to hang out at least one more time. The three friends went to the royal stable. There Prince Michael got on his prize possession, his horse, Lightning Speed. Waymond jumped on his horse, Tail feather, and poor Kelvin jumped on his lazy horse, Coach Roach.

"Get up!" Kelvin yelled at Coach Roach, but Coach Roach wouldn't move. Poor Kelvin had to run and catch up with Waymond; Waymond slowed down and helped Kelvin get on his horse.

They just had to ride through the countryside of the Ivory Tower one more time before they carried on their duties.

Prince Michael was known by the fair maidens of the Ivory Tower as Black Delight. This title suited him well, because he had beautiful dark skin and a statuesque figure that made the maidens go wild.

The maidens called Waymond, Black Dream and they called Kelvin, Black Wonder. Well Waymond, this guy had a way to sugar coat everything, and he was pleasing to the maiden's eyes.

Kelvin on the other hand, was more laid back. He looked like he hadn't eaten in days, but he too had his share of fair maidens. If you didn't have a cushion, well, you weren't for Kelvin.

The three rode their horses throughout the kingdom. All the maidens ran out, throwing kisses and holding their hearts, because Prince Michael and Waymond had truly enjoyed themselves before they fell in love with their princesses.

But for Kelvin, there were only two maidens throwing him kisses, it was May May. Kelvin liked maidens with meat on their bones. "I'm waiting my dear love!" May May yelled at Kelvin.

Then there was Lucky, she was over four hundred pounds, but her weight was distributed well. Kelvin loved Lucky, but he loved May May too. "Maybe I can have them both," Kelvin thought. But his thoughts were interrupted by his horse slowing down.

All three jumped off their horses and bowed their heads.

Also, Princess **Kimberly Dawn,** this lovely princess had the ability to change colors. This was fitting for royalty.

The Ivory princess fell in love with a prince and moved far away. She had two lovely children. One was black and the other one was Asian

I forgot to tell you about Kelly, he was close to the prince like a brother also, but Kelly wouldn't give up his guilty pleasures. He continued to surround himself with beautiful maidens. Another twist to this adventure, Kelly was also a prince. He was King Larry's brother from another mother. King Larry knew this, but Kelly didn't. But if he did, his head would've been even bigger than it already was. King Larry got tired of the rose maidens complaining about how Kelly broke their hearts. That's why he was banished, but the king gave Kelly two bags of silver.

Kelly continued to live his life like *there was no tomorrow.* Did Kelly change, maybe or maybe not?

.   Also, what about the children born that were rainbow-colored? Well, so far, I told you about the princess, Kimberly Dawn. When King Larry was sowing his oats, he fathered multiple children. His first-born, Brittany, was very poetic, but at one point in time, she lacked direction. She was white. Next, was Darnell, this nobleman could sing. He was a knight also but didn't use his skills unless absolutely necessary. When he got mad, he was mad. Their mother was a fair maiden named Kim. Darnell was light brown; they called Darnell, Black Hawk, because he could spot trouble a mile away. Then, there was, Lariyana, she was very skilled in concepts. Her skin was the color of rainbows. The youngest was name Jakari, he was just who he was, Jakari. I Almost forgot, Dalayna and Hannah, they had the same mother, but one was black and the other was white. All of King Larry's children were beautiful.

Now, let me see, I forgot to tell you about Queen Josephine sister's son, Jamey, they called him Black Trouble. Although he was probably the most gifted person of all, he couldn't get himself together. Black Trouble's mom died when he was young, but he didn't get to see the battles she had to face. You see, Jamey was in the dungeon, where the wicked queen resides now, and she couldn't stand Jamey, the one called Black Trouble. The wicked queen didn't have pity for him like her sister, the real queen. This troubled man just couldn't get *past his demons*. He surrounded himself with characters whose sole mission in life was to beat a dead horse. What I mean by that is, these characters blamed others for their shortcomings. Jamey was being used. If he only realized this, maybe he would have made better choices. But history will remember him as the most poetic being that ever walked the earth. Trouble used his talents in the dungeon to help negotiate, he saved the rat from a hungry bird, a bird from menacing cat, a cat from an angry dog, he negotiated until all in the dungeon had rights.

Little Mirror, resting in the sky, slowly closing his eyes. Then, there was a darkness that covered the sky. This was the first eclipse. So, when you see an eclipse, it's Little Mirror reflecting on his life on earth with a smile.

Princess Kimberly Dawn

Princess Teresa

Prince Michael

Spring

Fall

winter

Summer

Redoing Little mirror was a therapeutic experience because it allowed me to play with different characters and create different experiences.

A Child's Dream

Sweet honey drops of hope penetrated my heart, captivated by dreams of flowers, relaxing their blooms in the breeze of the midnight summer heat. Icicles filled with sweet plums melts in my mouth, as I think of a sunnier day, a day blistering from the summer heat.

Sparkles of rain scattered the ground with pleasurable things all around

As every year passes, a penny of hope remains because of the graceful beauty that is part of a child's dream.

To grow old with your love one, is the most unselfish and divine experience a person can ever hope to have

A timely love by Jamey Wilkins

Yesterday ended when today began

Tomorrow comes when today ends

Time started as soon as I was born

Forever seemed so far away

Eternity will start as soon as I'm gone

And tomorrow will always be today

Yesterday I fell in love with you

And tomorrow I will still be

Cause today I made a vow to love you until eternity

Forever is not long enough

Cause it ends as soon as I die

So until forever comes I want only you in my life

You meant the world to me yesterday

But today you mean much more

By the time tomorrow comes, I will love you even more than before. I
promise this through eternity, cause the only way I will depart

Is when the day comes you decide to break my heart

Don't ever leave me

Tomorrow will never come by Jamey Wilkins

It's like God licked his fingers

And put out my match

The match that lit my candle

The candle that sparked the lantern

The lantern that illuminated my room

Now I'm forever cloaked in darkness

Pitch black filled with gloom

Unless the sun decides to rise

Something we got to find the warrior inside and fight to reclaim our pride

When life become overwhelming, give yourself a moment to think about how blessed your life is.

If you help someone that is in need, your blessings will be multiplied not by men but by God

In redoing Little Mirror, I brought more definition to this little short story by showing that we are beautiful not by our outward appearance alone, but by the inner beauty that shines through and projects a glow that resonates exquisiteness. We are not compelled by what people dictate what beauty represents.

Because beauty comes in all colors, sometimes we prejudge others by their outward appearance not trying to see their inner beauty; it is that beauty that make each one of us unique.

If you want to read more adventures, it depends on you the audience!

If you do, here's a sneak preview

Prince Michael, Black Delight, he fights the Moss Ball King

His children: Princess Dasia, Teona and little Prince Bryson

They use their skills to fight for order and helped their father save his Kingdom, along with three of Prince Michael's trusted friends, Prince Waymond, Kelvin and Kelly

You wonder why Prince Michael wear shade, well, time will tell

Okay, he saw Little Mirror leave behind his mirror; he touched it causing a chain reaction, now the prince had powers equal to Little Mirror. He became the counterpart of Little Mirror.

April Shower

Sometimes I feel insignificant, like my existence has absolutely

No effect on the world. I am just a raindrop in on April

Shower rising, falling, spinning t each whim of the wind

Until finally I splash and cease to be I.

Support!

If you are looking for a used car, check out Carmania located at 2976 S. Church Street Rocky Mount NC, the owner, **Michael Hill** will find something for you that is reasonable and dependable (252) 382-0427

Jamil Burton, he created the book covering for Little Mirror. He did an excellent job. Contact number (252) 231-5565

For quality paintings and drawings contact jamiburtonart@gmail.com

If you are looking for an affectionate daycare, check out **St. Stephen's Loving Daycare at** 3861 n. Wesleyan Blvd, Rocky Mount NC 27804 (252)446 8756

Certified Teachers, no weekends, drop-off, 24 hrs. services, transportation and afterschool care

The Staff is friendly

Emma Trevathan hairdresser/actress contact her (252) 955-6943, she's would love to hear from you. This Lady is very talented!

Verner Avery (Clothes Doctor) for all your sewing and alteration needs located 100 NW Main Street Rocky Mount NC 27801

James Parker/director of Electric Image Band (252) 883-3122

For parties and gatherings, this band is outstanding!

Sophie Parker, she is the manager of a group called the Mighty Saint Steppers; they are exceptional! (252)314-4313

Sophie's team travels a lot, if you can support with a small donation

Sheritha Jackson amazing salon **Kut Above (Garner NC)**

Need Help call **Jesse Hinton Refrigeration and Appliances** (252) 985 3996

Finally, a woman that pushed me beyond my boundaries, my cousin and friend, Bettie Harrison

Sometimes we're not able to give financial support, but your time is equally important.

Also, check out Child Speak Out! and Priscilla's Smile by J. Bridgers

I ventured out and became my own publisher by revising all three books.

Always remember, when someone say you can't, prove you can!

Thank you for your support!

Let me give a shout out to Ms. Mary Mclain/Olive Hernandez

Quote by Lillian Jenkins *If you keep looking down at your feet you will never see the sunshine*

My father, Eddie Jenkins was a master storyteller, this gift resonated a desire that had to be explored

In memory of my husband's parents

Geneva and Charlie Bridgers

The Author

This journey wasn't easy becoming my own publisher, but when people say you can't, we must prove we can. When several doors are closed, there is one that is open.

Thanks to my mother Odell Jenkins,

Carrie and Jack Harrison, they opened the door for me